The Pyramid Cafe

Special Activities and Devotions For Teaching Nutrition

by Jane Jarrell and Deborah Saathoff

BROADMAN
& HOLMAN
PUBLISHERS

Published by Broadman & Holman Publishers, Nashville, Tennessee
Design: Katherine DeVault Design, Nashville, Tennessee

ISBN 0-8054-0361-2

Welcome to the Pyramid Cafe!

I am **Chef Nute Rition** and I will be your tour guide. Our tour of the Pyramid Cafe will be a fun and flavor-filled learning adventure. You see, the Pyramid Cafe is not just any restaurant. It's special because you don't just eat here, you find out why you eat and why what you eat is so important.

It's called the Pyramid Cafe because it's designed around the Food Pyramid. The Food Pyramid is a way of showing how much of what kinds of food we need to eat to keep our bodies healthy and working properly.

As we tour the Pyramid Cafe, you will study nutrition. Nutrition is learning about what God put inside our food and how our bodies use it. You'll also get to sample and enjoy some of the foods God has given us to keep our bodies working in tip-top shape.

So, come on in and let's begin!

Why Do You Need to Eat?

Before we get to the kitchen and the stations that prepare the foods, we're going to spend some time finding out why several times a day, every day of our lives, we put things in our mouths, chew them up, and swallow them.

> **Skin is completely replaced every seven years. If you're at least seven years old, you no longer have any of the skin you were born with!**

Why do we do this? Because we have to. Our bodies were designed by God to need fuel to keep going. Food is our fuel! And we need its energy to do all of the things we do every day from the time our eyes open in the morning until we go to bed at night. Even when still or sleeping, our bodies are always busy.

Here are some of the parts that need to keep going – even when you're sleeping: hair grows, nails grow, heart beats circulating blood, lungs breathe, brain makes sure everything is working properly, cuts and scrapes heal, stomach and intestines digest food, skin is replaced.

So how does the spaghetti, pizza, corn on the cob, or milkshake turn into hair, muscles, and skin? Through a process called digestion, your body takes the food you eat and breaks it down into chemical parts your body can use. These parts are called nutrients. Food begins to digest when you put it in your mouth and digestion ends when you go to the bathroom. In between, your body gets the nutrients it needs out of the food you have eaten.

Your body needs six main kinds of nutrients. Each nutrient has its own job in the body. The nutrients often work together and your body needs all of them, in the right amounts, to work the way God intended it to.

My helpers are here to explain what each nutrient does in your body. You are going to meet them throughout this book.

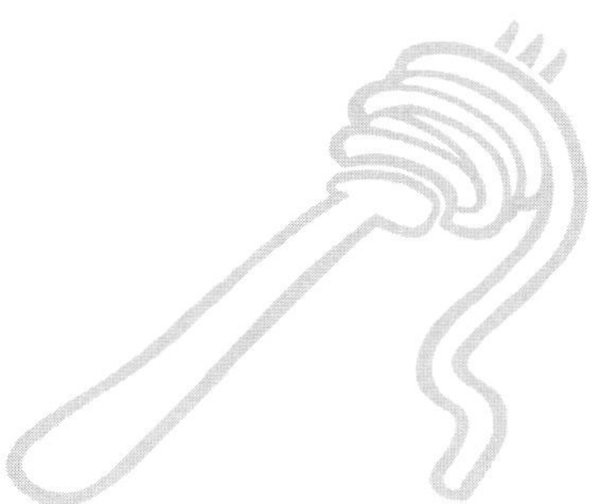

Meet Pro Tein

I'm **Pro Tein**. Almost three-fourths of your body's solid parts are made of protein: hair, muscles, bones, brain, fingernails, teeth, liver, and so on. Protein helps build these parts as you grow and helps repair the parts whenever they need it. Proteins work with other chemicals to help you breathe, digest your food, even think! Proteins also fight germs and help keep you healthy.

Your body gets protein from the food you eat. No plant, animal, or person can live without protein.

You have about 100,000 different kinds of protein in your body. All proteins are made of 20 building blocks called amino acids. Your body breaks the plant or animal protein in the food down into its amino acids. Then it rebuilds the amino acids into the kind of protein it needs for a specific job, like becoming a fingernail, muscle, or brain.

Endless Protein Possibilities Activity

So how can only 20 amino acids become 100,000 different proteins? Well, the English language only needs 26 letters to spell all the words in the entire language! This activity will help you see how that works.

Teacher's Note: Page 5 may be duplicated.

Things You'll Need:

- The 20 symbol blocks from page 5
- scissors
- paper
- pencil, pen, or crayon

Cut apart the 20 symbols below and record how many different combinations you can make. You may want to set a time limit because the possibilities are endless!

Devotion: *Dear God, help me remember that the same way eating good food makes my body strong, reading and studying the Bible will make my spirit strong. Thank You for giving me food for my body and Your Bible for my spirit.*

Like newborn babies, crave pure spiritual milk, so that by it you may grow up in your salvation.
1 Peter 2:2

Meet Vita Man

I'm **Vita Man**. Vitamins are found in food in very small amounts. Your body needs vitamins to grow, repair injuries like cuts and scrapes, stay healthy, and work properly.

To help you learn some of the important jobs vitamins do, let's play the Vitamin Game.

Vitamin Game Activity

No. of Players: 1 or more

Things You'll Need:

- One body outline for each player (see page 7; may be duplicated)
- One set of cards (may be duplicated and cut apart)
- Crayons or colored pencils for each player

Rules: Place the cards face down in a single stack. Players take turns drawing the cards. Each player colors the body part on the body outline that is mentioned on the card.

Some cards will duplicate the same body parts. The first child to color in all the illustrated body parts on the body outline wins.

Place each card on a discard pile as it is used. If the draw stack is used up before you have a body outline complete, shuffle the discard pile and begin drawing again from it.

Vitamin Game Cards

vitamin A needed for eyesight	**vitamin A** keeps skin smooth	**vitamin A** helps make hair form
vitamin A helps bones develop	**vitamin A** helps teeth develop	**vitamin D** keeps bones healthy
vitamin D keeps teeth healthy	**vitamin E** helps make blood cells	**vitamin E** helps make muscles
vitamin E helps make muscles	**vitamin K** keeps bones healthy	**vitamin C** keeps bones healthy
vitamin C keeps teeth healthy	**vitamin C** helps wounds heal	**vitamin C** keeps blood vessels healthy
vitamin C keeps skin smooth	**vitamin B6** helps form blood cells	**vitamin B6** helps nerves work properly
vitamin B3 keeps digestive system healthy	**vitamin B1** keeps nervous system healthy	**vitamin B1** helps change food to energy
vitamin B2 helps change food to energy	**vitamin B5** helps change food to energy	**vitamin B6** keeps nervous system healthy
folate (a B vitamin) helps body make blood cells	**vitamin B12** helps body make blood cells	**vitamin B12** helps keep nervous system healthy

VITAMIN GAME BODY OUTLINE

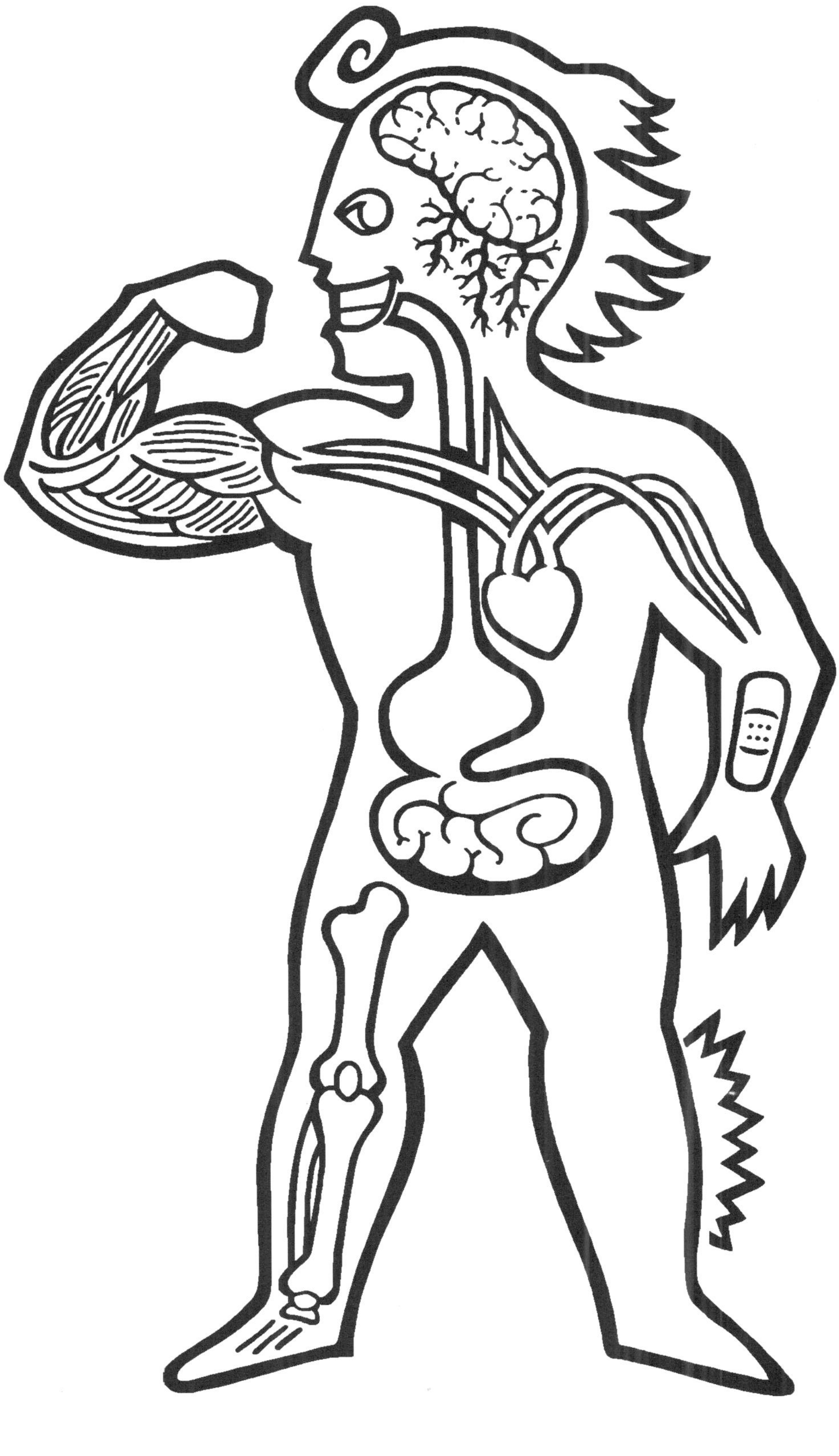

In case you're wondering what happened to vitamins F, G, H, and I, or why there are so many extra B's, here's why. Scientists get to name the vitamins they discover. The first ones discovered were given letter names in alphabetical order. They added the chemical names later. The researcher who discovered vitamin K lived in Denmark and he named it after the Danish word for clotting, koagulation. Vitamin K helps your blood clot so you stop bleeding after you get a cut or a scrape.

Meanwhile, scientists found out that what they thought was one vitamin B was really a whole group of vitamins that are usually found together in the same foods. So they put numbers with the B. By the time the last B vitamins were discovered, the letter-naming system was out of style, so they just have chemical names.

Devotion: *Dear God, thank You for making sure that the foods You've given us have everything we need to keep our amazing bodies working so well.*

I praise you because I am fearfully and wonderfully made; your works are wonderful, I know that full well. ***Psalm 139:14***

Keep These Assistants In Balance

I'm **Minnie Ral**. A mineral is anything God made that isn't a plant or an animal. Rocks are minerals! You don't eat rocks, but your body does need about 20 different kinds of minerals, in very tiny amounts, to work properly.

Minerals are your body's building materials for bones, blood, and teeth. They help your muscles work, your blood clot, and your heart beat. They help carry messages to the brain and help your blood carry the oxygen from your lungs to all the parts of your body.

I'm **Fiber**. Fiber is the nutrient your body needs but can't digest. It works like a garbage truck for your body. Fiber picks up the waste that's left after you've digested the food's nutrients and keeps the food waste moving through your digestive system and out through your bowels when you go to the bathroom.

I'm **Carbo Hydrate**.

Carbohydrates are your body's fuel. They give your body the energy it needs to do all its many jobs.

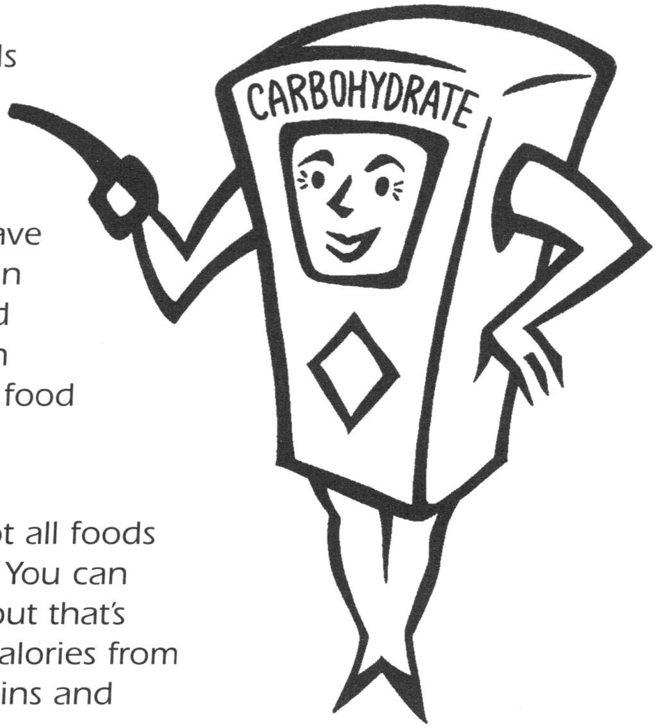

We measure how much energy a food has in units called calories. All foods have calories, but some foods have more than others. Nutrition experts have measured the calories in all sorts of food. You can get that information from the labels on food cans, jars, and packages.

Even though all foods have calories, not all foods contain the nutrients your body needs. You can get 270 calories from a chocolate bar, but that's all you'll get. You'll get the same 270 calories from a piece of chicken and it contains proteins and vitamins as well.

I'm **Fats**. Like carbohydrates, fats are energy-givers, too. They're also needed in small amounts to help bodies grow.

If you put more fuel in a car's gas tank than it will hold, the extra fuel will spill out on the ground. Your body keeps all the extra calories you eat, though, and stores them as fat. When you need more energy, you will either give your body more food or it will use the stored fat. If you eat more than your body needs for a long period of time, your body will store too much fat. If you don't eat enough food for a long period of time, your body will use up all the stored fat and you'll be too thin. Being too fat or too thin is bad for your health.

Balancing Act Worksheet

Try this balancing act to see how much energy is needed to do some familiar activities for one hour and what foods give the needed calories. See how closely you can get the numbers to match, or balance, on each side (you can't always be exact).

Materials needed:

- This worksheet ▪ A calculator
- Activities & foods listed below and worksheet on page 12

Choose 3 or 4 activities. Place them on the right side of the scale. Add the calories together for all the activities. Now choose from the food chart and write them on the left side of the scale. Add the calories together and see how closely you can make the activity number and the food number match. Remember, the more activities you can do, the more foods you can choose!

Activities:

watching television: 85
reading: 85
writing: 115
bicycling: 600
soccer: 650
tennis: 450
basketball: 550
jogging: 600
hiking: 400
jumping rope: 750
swimming: 275
sleeping: 60
studying: 130
piano playing: 190
lawn mowing: 460

Foods:

hamburger: 270
4 oz. roasted chicken: 200
cheeseburger: 320
1 slice pepperoni pizza: 370
10 french fries: 220
grilled cheese sandwich: 450
peanut butter and jelly sandwich: 330
1 oz. chocolate candy bar: 160
1 donut: 210
1 apple: 80
1 banana: 105
8 oz. yogurt: 230
1 iced cupcake: 130
1 fried chicken drumstick: 120
8 oz. glass whole milk: 160
12 oz. can of soda: 155
1 cup of grapes: 60
1 cup of green beans: 30
1 cup of broccoli: 40
1 raw carrot: 20
1 stick of gum: 10
1 cup of chili: 170
1 cup of cauliflower: 25
1 medium tomato: 40
1 ear of corn: 70

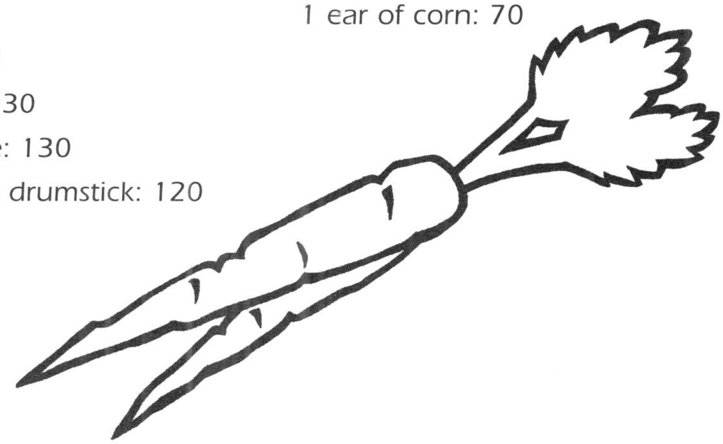

Balancing Act Worksheet

Foods

Activities

Breads, Cereals, Rice, and Pasta

The first station in our tour of the Pyramid Cafe is the base of the pyramid, the part all the others are built on: **Breads, Cereal, Rice, and Pasta**. We need more of these kinds of foods than any other kind. The Bible tells us that God had the Israelites take bread with them when they left Egypt. Jesus often shared bread with His friends. One of His miracles made two loaves of bread feed over 5,000 people! His last supper on earth included bread, so bread is a part of the communion we share at church.

The foods you find here have **carbohydrates** in them but not much fat, so they're the body's favorite fuel. They give you lots of energy!

These foods are a good source of important **B vitamins** which help you grow.

They have **minerals**.

And **fiber** too! Especially if you look for whole grain foods.

People today don't usually eat the whole kernel of grains with the exception of rice and corn. We usually grind, or mill, the grains. We make flour for breads, cakes, crackers, cookies, pancakes, waffles, and pasta by grinding the kernel.

Breads, Cereals, Rice & Pasta: cornbread, rye, pumpernickel, potato, French, Italian, sourdough, pita, oatmeal, wheat and white breads, bagels, biscuits, buns, cake, cereals, cookies, crackers, croissants, doughnuts, macaroni, muffins, pancakes, pastries, pies, dark and white rice, rolls, spaghetti, tortillas, and waffles

Devotion: *Dear God, thank You for bread that's so important for our bodies. Thank You for Jesus, our spirit's bread of life."*

Then Jesus declared, "I am the bread of life. He who comes to me will never go hungry, and he who believes in me will never be thirsty. ***John 6:35***

6 to 11 servings recommended daily.
One serving =
1 slice of bread;
1 ounce of cereal;
1/2 hamburger bun;
1/2 cup cooked rice

Recipes

Honey Whole Wheat Bread

Things You'll Need:

• 2 medium (8 1/2 x 4 1/2) loaf pans, greased (don't use shiny aluminum pans) • small bowl
• large bowl • measuring cups and spoons • wooden spoon • brush
• vegetable oil • plastic wrap • wax paper • wire racks

Ingredients:

1 package dry yeast
1/4 cup warm water (105° - 115°)
2 cups hot water (120° - 130°)
3 tablespoons shortening
3 tablespoons honey
2 cups whole wheat flour
1/2 cup instant potatoes
1/2 cup non-fat dry milk
1 1/2 tablespoons salt
3 - 4 cups all-purpose white flour

If you'd like to try a few of the recipes we use at the Pyramid Cafe, here are some **Breads, Cereals, Rice,** and **Pasta** recipes!

1. Dissolve yeast in the warm water in the small bowl.
2. In the large mixing bowl, measure hot water, shortening, and honey. Stir to blend. Add the whole wheat flour, instant potatoes, milk, and salt. Pour in the yeast mixture and blend well.
3. With the wooden spoon, stir in the all-purpose flour, 1/2 cup at a time, to make a rough ball of dough that leaves the sides of the bowl. Use your fingers when the dough gets too thick and stiff to be stirred by the spoon.
4. Sprinkle flour on a counter top or board and turn the dough out onto it. Knead the dough until it makes a smooth, stretchy ball (about 8 minutes.) Add a little flour if the dough sticks to your hands or work surface.
5. Put the dough back in the bowl. Brush with vegetable oil and cover the bowl tightly with plastic wrap. Put in a warm place (80° - 85°) until it has doubled in size. To see if the dough is ready, stick two fingers into the dough, if the dent stays, the dough is ready. This will take about an hour to an hour and a half.
6. Punch the dough down by plunging your fist deep into the center of the dough.
7. Turn the dough out onto the counter and separate it into two equal halves. Shape each half into a ball and let it stand 5 minutes.
8. Flatten each ball into an oval about as wide as the long side of your baking pans. Fold the oval in half, pinch the seam together tightly, and plump into a loaf-shape with the seam on the bottom. Put each loaf in a pan.
9. Cover the pans with wax paper and put in a warm place until the dough has doubled in volume or reached an inch or so above the edge of the pan. Lightly press the top edge of the loaf with your finger. If the impression remains then the dough is ready to bake. It will take about 45 minutes.
10. Preheat the oven to 400°. Place the pans in the oven. When the loaves are a light brown and tapping the bottom crust makes a hard and hollow sound, they are done. This will take about 45 to 50 minutes.
11. Remove bread from the oven, turn loaves out of the pans onto wire racks to cool.

Five Layer Pasta Parfaits *Serves 4*

> Money is sometimes called "bread" because the ancient Egyptians who first baked bread like we enjoy today valued it so much, it could be used to purchase things as a form of money.

Things You'll Need:
•saucepans • colander • 4 parfait glasses
• measuring cups and spoons

Ingredients:
1/2 pound of each of three different pastas: red, yellow, and green
1/2 cup Parmesan cheese, grated
1 cup mixed vegetables, diced and cooked
1 cup prepared Alfredo sauce
4 garlic bread sticks
1 tablespoon Parmesan cheese, grated

1. Prepare the three different pastas separately according to package directions. Drain and set aside.
2. Layer the ingredients as follows: 1 color pasta, Parmesan cheese, 2nd color pasta, mixed vegetables, Parmesan cheese, 3rd color pasta.
3. Heat the prepared Alfredo sauce in the microwave and spoon it over each parfait.
4. Top with Parmesan cheese and place the bread stick in as a garnish, to look like a straw.

Crazy Colorful Cooked Cereal *Makes 5 cups*

Things You'll Need:
• 13x9x2-inch glass baking dish • saucepan • measuring cups and spoons • spatula

Ingredients:
1 cup quick-cooking oats
1/2 cup whole-bran cereal
1/2 cup whole wheat flour
1/4 cup (1/2 stick) butter
1/2 cup honey
1 teaspoon vanilla extract
1/2 teaspoon almond extract
1/2 cup dried apricots, chopped
1/2 cup golden raisins
1/4 cup dried cranberries

1. Preheat the oven to 300 degrees.
2. Mix oats, cereal, and flour together in an ungreased 13x9x2-inch baking dish.
3. Heat butter and honey until hot and bubbling; stir in vanilla and almond extracts.
4. Pour the honey mixture over the oat mixture; stir thoroughly to combine.
5. Bake until light brown, about 30 to 35 minutes.
6. Stir in dried apricots, raisins, and cranberries. Cool.
7. Loosen granola from the pan with a spatula.
   Break the granola into pieces.
   Store in an airtight container.

> If bread had feet, do you know what kind of shoes it would wear? Loafers!

Vegetables

Welcome to our next stop on our tour of the Pyramid Cafe: **Vegetables!** Not only did God give us so many plants to eat, we eat lots of parts of those plants as well. You see, a vegetable is part of a plant that we usually eat with the main part of our meal. We eat the leaves, stems and stalks, flowers, fruits, seeds, bulbs, and roots of all kinds of plants. They are absolutely necessary for your body to stay healthy. You don't have to eat every vegetable to be healthy, but you do need to eat many different ones.

Vegetables have lots of important **vitamins**, especially vitamins A and C.

Vegetables are a great source of **fiber**!

Leafy vegetables have lots of **calcium, iron,** and **magnesium**.

You'll find **carbohydrates** in some vegetables.

And **proteins** too!

5 Servings Recommended.
One serving = 1/2 cup cooked vegetables, 1 cup raw vegetables, or 3/4 cup of vegetable juice.

▪ **Leafy Vegetables:**
spinach, cabbage, Brussels sprouts, kale, parsley, lettuce, mustard, collard, beet and turnip greens, arugula

▪ **Vegetable Stalks:**
celery, asparagus, rhubarb, kohlrabi, fennel, chive

▪ **Vegetable Flowers:**
cauliflower, broccoli, artichoke

▪ **Vegetable Fruit:**
tomatoes, cucumbers, summer and winter squash, eggplant, peppers, kidney beans, green beans, lima beans, navy beans, green peas, black-eyed peas, chick peas, okra, pumpkin

▪ **Vegetable Root:**
carrot, parsnip, turnip, rutabaga, beets, radish, celeriac, Jerusalem artichoke, potato, sweet potato, yam, peanut

▪ **Vegetable Bulbs:** onion, garlic, scallion

▪ **Vegetable Seeds:** peas.

Power Produce: the most nutritious vegetables are: broccoli, spinach, peppers (especially red), sweet potatoes, onions, tomatoes.

Sources of vitamin A: carrots, sweet potatoes, pumpkins, broccoli, spinach, beet greens, chard, chicory, turnip greens and kale.
Sources of Vitamin B-complex (folate): spinach, cabbage, Brussels sprouts, romaine and loose-leaf lettuce, okra, sweet corn, beets, cauliflower.
Sources of Vitamin C: broccoli, cauliflower, peppers, potatoes, tomatoes.
Sources of Vitamin E: leafy vegetables.
Sources of vitamin K: turnip greens, cauliflower, broccoli, cabbage, lettuce, spinach, asparagus.
Sources of calcium: kale, mustard greens, turnip greens, pak-choi.
Sources of iron: broccoli, kale, turnip greens, collards.
Sources of magnesium: green, leafy vegetables, legumes like beans and peas.

One Potato, Two Potato, Three Potato, Four

We eat potatoes fixed in more different ways than any other vegetable. But it hasn't always been that way. When Europeans first brought potatoes back from Peru, where they were first grown, people didn't want to have anything to do with them. They thought they were ugly lumps. Now the French call them pommes de terre which means "apples of the earth" and the average American eats over 120 pounds of potatoes each year! We even play a game called "Hot Potato." You can try it yourself.

Hot Potato Game

Things You'll Need: ▪ one large potato
▪ music (instrument, radio, or cassette tape)

Children should stand in a circle with one child holding the potato. Start the music and pass the potato around until the music stops. The child holding the potato sits down and the others continue until only one child is left.

Potato Experiment

Potatoes are full of nutrients such as **vitamin C** and **fiber**. We boil, mash, bake, steam, roast, and fry them; eat them hot and cold; eat them whole, cut up, and mashed. Try this experiment to learn how potatoes grow.

Things You'll Need:

▪ a potato with at least 2 or 3 "eyes" or oval-shaped depressions in the potato's skin
▪ a glass jar, wide enough to allow the potato to drop in lengthwise, almost filled with water ▪ about a half-dozen toothpicks

Place the potato halfway into the jar of water using the toothpicks to hold it in place. Keep your potato away from direct sunlight for about a week. Once you see leaves and roots sprouting, put your potato in a sunny spot. When the plant is about 6 or 8 inches tall, plant it in a flower pot.

Devotion: *Dear God, thank You for teaching us that, like potatoes, what makes a person special isn't what we see on the outside but what comes from the inside, like our thoughts, feelings, words, and actions.*

But the LORD said to Samuel, "Do not consider his appearance or his height, for I have rejected him. The LORD does not look at the things man looks at. Man looks at the outward appearance, but the LORD looks at the heart." ***1 Samuel 16:7***

Vegetable Variety Activity

It's important to eat many different kinds, or a variety, of vegetables. This activity will help you find out if you're getting a good vegetable variety in your diet!

Things You'll Need:

▪ This page ▪ The Pyramid Cafe's vegetable list on page 16 ▪ A pencil

Write the vegetables you eat in the space where it belongs. Write the vitamins or minerals the vegetable gives you next to its name.

leaves	flowers	seeds	fruit	stalks and stems	roots	bulbs

Do you have a variety, or a lot of different kinds, of vegetables on your chart?

If not, identify 2 or 3 vegetables from our kitchen you think you'd like to try. Or, try our Pyramid Cafe recipes on the next two pages to add to your list!

Devotion: *Dear God, You've given us so many wonderful plants to enjoy and to eat. Thank You for thinking of so many kinds and giving them to us.*

Then God said, "I give you every seed-bearing plant on the face of the whole earth and every tree that has fruit with seed in it. They will be yours for food. ***Genesis 1:29***

When you eat broccoli, you're eating a bunch of flowers! A head of broccoli is a group of buds about to flower.

The first carrots eaten over 3,000 years ago were white, purple, and yellow. Orange carrots weren't developed until the 1600's by the Dutch.

What do you call a spinach that insults a farmer? A fresh vegetable!

Double Smashed Potatoes *Serves 6*

Things You'll Need:

• vegetable peeler • paring knife • large saucepan • electric blender • electric mixer• a liquid measuring cup • measuring cups and spoons • stove or hot plate

Ingredients:

4 large white potatoes,
   peeled and cut into cubes
2 medium sweet potatoes,
   peeled and cut into cubes
1 cup cottage cheese
1 cup milk
2 tablespoons butter
teaspoon salt

1. In a large saucepan cover the potatoes with cold water. Bring to a boil, and cook for about 15 minutes, or until tender.
2. While the potatoes are cooking place the milk and the cottage cheese in a blender, blend until liquefied.
3. Drain the potatoes and return them to the pot, with an electric mixer, mash the potatoes until almost smooth.
4. Turn the heat on low and stir in the cottage cheese mixture. Add butter, salt and pepper to taste.

Celery was given as prizes for athletic contests in ancient Greece.

Pumpkin Pals *Makes 6 to 8 pals*

Things You'll Need:

• measuring cups and spoons • spoons for stirring • bowl • large skillet

Ingredients:

2 cups biscuit mix
2 tablespoons brown sugar
2 teaspoons cinnamon
1 teaspoon allspice
1 cup milk
1 cup pumpkin
2 tablespoons oil
2 eggs
1 teaspoon vanilla
small package of raisins

Ancient Greeks and Romans believed asparagus helped prevent bee stings and relieved the pain of toothaches.

1. Combine all ingredients in a medium bowl, stir to combine.
2. Pour enough oil in a large skillet to coat the bottom of the pan.
3. Using a cup measure scoop out the batter and pour into the skillet. Cook 2 minutes on one side and flip to the other side and cook another 2 minutes or until browned.
4. Make a face for your pal using the raisins. Serve with butter and maple syrup.

Fruits

Welcome to the **Fruits** station on our tour of the Pyramid Cafe! You may have noticed that every stop so far has been a product of a plant: the grains, vegetables, and now fruits. The Food Pyramid has plant foods at the base because scientists have proven that plant foods like grains, vegetables, and fruits, need to be the foundation of our diets. That doesn't mean we shouldn't eat anything else. It just means God designed our bodies to need more plant foods than animal foods like meat and milk.

FRUITS

apples, avocado, apricot, banana, blackberries, blueberries, cantaloupe, cherries, cranberries, dates, figs, gooseberries, grapefruit, grapes, honeydew melon, kiwifruit, lemon, lime, mango, nectarine, orange, papaya, peach, pear, pineapple, plums, prunes, raisins, raspberries, rhubarb, strawberries, tangerine, watermelon

Because cucumbers, eggplants, peppers, tomatoes, squash, peas, beans, and pumpkins aren't sweet, we call them vegetables. But they're really fruits. The part of a plant that has seeds in it is always the fruit. Any other part–the leaves, the root, or the stalk–is the vegetable.

2-3 Servings a Day. 1 serving = 1 piece of medium fruit, 1/2 cup of canned or chopped fruits or berries, or 1/2 cup of fruit juice.

Eating fruits is a great way to get important **vitamins** like A and D.

Fruits have a lot of fructose, a natural sugar that has **carbohydrates**, so they're a good source of energy.

Fruits have a lot of **fiber** to help your digestive system stay healthy.

Bananas have a lot of potassium, an important **mineral** your body needs.

Raisins first became popular after a heat wave dried a grape crop on the vine in California's San Joaquin Valley in 1870.

Lemons were first sold in the United States during the California Gold Rush in 1849. Miners drank lemon juice to keep from getting scurvy, a disease caused by a lack of vitamin C.

Apple Appeal Activity

Try this experiment to find out how to keep your bananas appealing, even when they're peeled!

Bananas are the most popular fruit in America. We eat over 4 million tons of them every year!

Things You'll Need:

▪ An apple ▪ A knife ▪ Orange juice▪A small bowl ▪ Two plates

Pour the orange juice into the bowl. Cut the apple in half. Slice each half into an equal number of pieces about the same size. Put the slices from one half on a plate. Put the slices from the other half into the orange juice. Make sure they are completely covered. Remove the slices from the juice and put on the second plate. Compare the two plates after an hour or two. What has happened to the apple slices that were not dipped in orange juice?

When fruit is sliced, especially apples, peaches, pears, and bananas, oxygen, a chemical in the air, causes chemicals in the fruit to make it turn brown. We call this oxidation. Vitamin C is an antioxidant, it stops the oxygen from reacting with the fruit's chemicals. You can dip sliced fruit in any juice that contains vitamin C: orange, pineapple, or lemon juices, to prevent browning.

Fruit that has turned brown is still good to eat, even if it is discolored.

Sources of vitamin C: citrus fruits like oranges, lemons, limes, cranberries, cantaloupe, strawberries
Sources of vitamin A: mango, papaya, cantaloupe, apricots
Sources of vitamin B-complex (folate): blackberries, boysenberries, kiwifruit, oranges, plantains, strawberries, orange juice and pineapple juice;
Source of potassium: bananas

Sweet and Sour Activity

The sweet apple juice you enjoy at snack time is the same apple juice companies use to make sour vinegar used in salad dressings! You can try this activity to see how it happens, but you have to be patient–it takes several days. While you wait, do you know what side of an apple is the reddest? The outside!

Things You'll Need:

▪ 1 cup of apple juice ▪ 2 jars or drinking glasses
▪ 1 box of baking soda

1. Pour the apple juice into a glass or jar. Leave it on a counter but don't cover it.
2. Each day test the apple juice for vinegar by putting 2 or 3 teaspoons of apple juice into the second glass or jar. Add a pinch of baking soda to the second glass. If it foams or bubbles when the baking soda is added, you have vinegar.
3. Repeat step 2 until you see foam.

Devotion: *Dear God, Your Bible tells us that Your words are always sweet when we study them and learn from them. Thank You for sweetness that lasts forever.*

How sweet are your words to my taste, sweeter than honey to my mouth! ***Psalm 119:103***

Fruit and Veggie Art Activity

The outside of a strawberry is covered with 200 tiny seeds.

Here's your chance to be creative with fruits and vegetables without eating them!

Things You'll Need:

- assorted fruits and vegetables ▪ knife ▪ thick, water soluble paint
- thick paintbrushes or sponges ▪ construction paper

1. Cut a section from a vegetable or fruit, look at any seeds inside. Try to find fruits and vegetables that have interesting shapes.
2. Use a thick brush or sponge to cover the cut surface of the vegetable or fruit with the paint.
3. Press the vegetable or fruit paint-side down onto a sheet of colored construction paper to make a print. Try making a pattern using different shapes.

Mangos are the most popular fruit in the world.

Ripe Bananas Activity

Why are bananas so attractive? Because they have plenty of a-peel! Bananas are just one of many fruits that continue to ripen even after they're picked from the plant. Try this experiment to see if you can get fruit to ripen more quickly.

Things You'll Need:

- 2 not-quite-ripe bananas (look for green color) of about the same color and size
- a paper or plastic bag with a few small holes poked in it

1. Leave one banana out on a table or counter. Put the other banana in the bag.
2. Check the color of the bananas each morning for 3 days.

Which banana ripened (and turned black) the fastest?

Devotion: *Dear God, help me to live my life so that I am not changed by the bad things around me but so that I can help others see Your goodness in me.*

"You are the light of the world. . .let you light shine in front of others. Then they will see the good things you do. And they will praise your Father who is in heaven." ***Matthew 5:14a, 16.***

Christopher Columbus brought pineapples as a gift to Queen Isabella in 1493.

Dairy

Welcome to the fourth station in our tour of the Pyramid Cafe! Here we find all of the **Dairy** foods, like milk, ice cream, yogurt, and cheese.

The foods you find here are packed with **minerals**.

Don't forget those great **vitamins** in the dairy section will help your body stay healthy with lots of vitamin A and D.

It is an excellent source of calcium, the bone builder that is so important to the body during our growing years. Even after we stop growing the bones, muscles, nerves, blood, and skeleton need a regular supply of calcium.

The same milk that helps our bones and teeth also gives us the **protein** needed for making and repairing body tissue. So if you get hurt, you'll sure be glad if you're full of milk. Milk comes in second to meat as our main source of protein.

2-3 servings recommended. One serving is equal to a cup of milk or yogurt or 1 ounce of cheese.

Dairy
buttermilk,
whole milk,
skim milk,
chocolate milk,
evaporated milk,
cheese, yogurt
sour cream,
cream cheese,
whipped cream,
butter, ice cream

Milk was the first food you were given after birth. As you grew, you began to eat other foods too, but milk probably remained the single most important item in your diet.

Milk is such a good food that it is very important that you drink lots of it. The same milk you pour on your breakfast cereal is also used to make butter and cheese and is cooked in dessert puddings. I'll bet you can think of something cold and creamy that is made of milk? (A hint: I scream you scream we all scream for ice cream.)

Many of the earliest known historical writings refer to milk. People were milking animals before anyone began writing history. Many believe that the people of Southwest Asia were the ones who first began taking special care of animals in order to collect their milk.

Devotion: *Dear God, Thank You for always taking care of us. Thank You for Your Bible and its stories of how You've taken care of Your people for thousands and thousands of years.*

The LORD said, "I have indeed seen the misery of my people in Egypt. I have heard them crying out because of their slave drivers, and I am concerned about their suffering. So I have come down to rescue them from the hand of the Egyptians and to bring them up out of that land into a good and spacious land, a land flowing with milk and honey. ***Exodus 3:7-8***

One of the first things ever discovered about milk is that it separates if allowed to stand undisturbed for a few hours. A yellowish layer floats to the surface leaving a bluish-white layer beneath. The yellow layer is a collection of bits of fat that are lighter than the rest of milk and rise to the top. If shaken vigorously, it forms a soft yellow substance called butter.

Today we have a process called homogenization that keeps the butterfat evenly distributed throughout the milk. This is why the milk you see is all one color.

Milk can change into all different types of things. If left to dry, it forms a spreadable paste called cream cheese which isn't a cheese at all, but dried cream.

Milk contains many different types of bacteria. Some of these bacteria are used to make yogurt and cheese. When the bacteria in the milk begins to grow it changes the milk.

The Great Change Activity:

Things You'll Need:

▪ cup of at least two of the following kinds of milk: skim milk, powdered milk, chocolate milk, or boxed, evaporated milk ▪ cup of whole milk ▪ cup whole milk that has been boiled for 10 to 15 minutes ▪ 2 to 6 small bottles with tops (clean jelly jars or baby food jars will work) ▪ 1 teaspoon ▪ tape ▪ small strips of paper for labels ▪ 1 pencil or pen

Caution: Do not attempt to drink the milk that has been set out on the counter after this experiment.

1. Place about 8 teaspoons of the boiled milk in a jar and cover the jar. Label the jar "boiled."
2. Place about 8 teaspoons of whole milk into one jar. Cover the jar and label this jar "whole milk."
3. Place about 8 teaspoons of at least one other kind of milk into a different jar. Cover the jar and label what kind of milk you used. Do this step for the many different types of milk you use.
4. Put all of the jars on a table or counter and let them sit in the room.
5. Place 8 teaspoons of refrigerated milk in another jar. Cover the jar and label it "refrigerator." Refrigerate.
6. Look at each jar each day and describe what the milk looks like. Has it begun to get solid? Has it begun to smell? How does it smell? Write down what you see and smell each day.
   Do step 6 at least every day for one week.

***Devotion:** Dear God, thank You for creating differences. Even though You made us all different colors, shapes, and sizes, You made us the same on the inside. We all need the same vitamins, minerals and nutrients for our bodies. Our hearts all need the same love, kindness, and caring.*

Do not show partiality to the poor or favoritism to the great, but judge your neighbor fairly. Do not seek revenge or bear a grudge against one of your people, but love your neighbor as yourself. I am the LORD. ***Leviticus 19:15b,18***

The Food Pyramid

So whether you eat or drink or whatever you do, do it all for the glory of God. **1 Corinthians 10:31**

Eating Healthy

What do the food experts say? Well, the food experts at the United States Department of Agriculture and Health and Human Services suggest that we:

- Eat a variety of foods
- Maintain a healthy body weight
- Choose a diet low in fat, saturated fat, and cholesterol.
- Choose a diet with plenty of vegetables, fruits and grain products
- Use sugar in moderation
- Use salt in moderation

A man can do nothing better than to eat and drink and find satisfaction in his work. This too, I see, is from the hand of God, for without him, who can eat or find enjoyment? ***Ecclesiastes 2:24-25***

Frozen Whipped Cream

Things You'll Need:
• medium bowl • spoon • measuring spoon • ice tray

Ingredients:
whipping cream
powdered sugar
vanilla

1. In a medium bowl combine, whipping cream, powdered sugar and vanilla.
2. Stir to combine, lightly spray a ice tray with cooking spray, pour cream into ice tray and place in freezer until frozen.
3. Remove the frozen cream by gently twisting the ice tray. Serve on warm apple pie or hot brownies.

Just how does what the cow eats become milk? God created a wonderfully complex digestive system in the cow. Did you know that a cow has four stomachs?

The cow is able to change huge amounts of water and vegetables such as grass and clover, which humans can't eat, into one of man's most important foods.

I wonder how a brown cow that eats green grass
gives white milk that can make yellow butter? Hmmm!

The taste of milk varies according to what the animal eats and drinks. If a cow feeds on rich summer grass, its milk will also be rich. If a cow eats a lot of a certain plant, then the milk will taste like the plant. The food and the milk made from it, will be different depending on the place, the season, and the weather.

Devotion: *Dear God, thank You for making all the living creatures You've given to us for food.*

God made the wild animals according to their kinds, the livestock according to their kinds, and all the creatures that move along the ground according to their kinds. And God saw that it was good. Then God said, "Let us make man in our image, in our likeness, and let them rule over the fish of the sea and the birds of the air, over the livestock, over all the earth, and over all the creatures that move along the ground." ***Genesis 1:25-26***

The cow is the main milk-giving animal in the world, and cows produce more milk for human use than all other milk givers together. But, do you know why cows dance? To make their milkshakes.

Milk must be cleaned before we can drink it. A French chemist by the name of Louis Pasteur invented a process called pasteurization. This is a process where the milk is heated but not boiled. This kills any harmful organisms without changing the flavor of the milk. It also makes it safe to drink.

Moo-ving right along, there are many types, names, and flavors of milk.

"Dairy Day" Activity

Things You'll Need:

▪ paper cups ▪ knives ▪ crackers ▪ napkins
▪ paper ▪ pencils

Have a "Dairy Day". If you are working in a classroom ask each child to bring a specific dairy product. Place all of the dairy items on a table and have a taste test. Rate the items you like from best to worst and discuss your results and how the product was made.

Use the milk products listed below as part of your "dairy day". Take a look at each of these kinds of milk and discuss the differences found from one kind to another.

(Note to teacher: You may want to divide this activity into two days, one with a variety of dairy products and one focusing on milks.)

▪ Whole milk ▪ Powdered milk ▪ Skim milk ▪ Sweetened Condensed Milk ▪ Buttermilk ▪ Evaporated milk ▪ Acidophilous milk ▪ Cream ▪ Yogurt

Devotion: *Dear God, thank You for all of the special ways milk can be used. Not only is it good for us it helps us to make so many different and delicious things. Help me each day to realize how wonderful You are.*

My flesh and my heart may fail, but God is the strength of my heart and my portion forever.
Psalm 73:26

Butter is an edible animal **fat**, made from milk and cream which have been made solid by churning (or stirring).

Butter can be made from fresh or slightly acid milk (this affects the taste and the spreading consistency) and it can be salted or sweetened. Butter has been a basic food since men began wandering to find pasture for their animals.

Butter has been around forever; it was known to the ancient world as a symbol of good and plenty. The Romans used it as a medicine. The Bible is full of Scriptures about butter: Judges 5:25, Job 29:6, Psalm 55:21, Proverbs 30:33 and Isaiah 7:15-22.

Butter probably originated by surprise when the milk of animals was carried in food containers, churned itself during the travels of the nomads.

Homemade Butter

Things You'll Need:
- measuring cup • measuring spoons
- container with a screw top lid

Ingredients:
- 1 cup cream • teaspoon salt

1. Place the cream and salt in a container with screw-on lid.
2. Screw the lid on tightly, and roll the jar back and forth with someone until the mixture turns to butter. Be prepared to roll for a while.
3. Drain off excess liquid and serve (or refrigerate until snack time).

Devotion: *Your choices matter. If you do what is right you will produce something usable, like butter, but if you do something wrong, you will get something wrong. So what you do and say affects you and others around you.*

For as churning the milk produces butter, and as twisting the nose produces blood, so stirring up anger produces strife." ***Proverbs 30:33***

Cream can be sweet or sour. Sour cream in its simplest form is unpasteurized heavy sweet cream that has been allowed to stand in a warm place until it has become sour. This method of souring cream gives a product that is different each time. The sour cream that is sold in the grocery stores is made from sweet cream that is chemically treated with lactic-acid bacteria to give a thick cream with a tangy flavor.

Cream cheese is really heavy cream that is dried, but not soured. Cream cheese is used on bagels, in cheesecakes, and in dips.

Making Cream Cheese

Things You'll Need:

- small shallow cardboard box or lid (make sure the box is not waxed or covered with coated paper, moisture must be able to seep through it.)
- piece of cloth or handkerchief ▪ wire rack ▪ 1 pint heavy cream

1. Line the box with the cloth.
2. Pour a half-inch layer of heavy cream into the box.
3. Allow the cream to stand at room temperature for a day or two. (This lets the moisture evaporate from the cream through the cardboard, leaving behind only the bits of butterfat.)
4. Within a couple of days the cream will have dried enough so that it can be spread, but it will not yet be sour. To remove from box, carefully lift the cloth from the box.

Ice cream is made from the rich fatty part of whole milk. The longer cream stands the thicker it will be. There are different kinds of cream depending on how much butterfat is in them.

Can you guess some of the major ingredients in ice cream? Cream, milk, sugar, and flavoring. You will never guess one of the most important ingredients: plain, unflavored, uncolored air. Air is stirred into ice cream as it freezes. Without the air, eating ice cream would be like chewing milky ice cubes.

Homemade Ice Cream

Things You'll Need:
• plastic jug • 1 Dixie™ cup • 1 Styrofoam™ cup • 2 stir sticks
• thermometer that can measure below freezing

Ingredients:
2 cups cream
1 cup sugar
teaspoon vanilla
clean snow or finely crushed ice
4 tablespoons salt

1. Mix the cream, sugar, and vanilla together in the jug.
2. Pour some cream mixture into the Dixie™ cup, filling it half to 3/4 full. Keep it cold.
3. Fill the Styrofoam™ cup full with snow or ice. If you have a thermometer measure the temperature of the ice.
4. Add about 3 to 4 tablespoons of salt to the ice. Stir. (Mark the stir stick you use so you will not use it in the ice cream mix.) Measure the temperature of the ice again.
5. Make a hole in the icy slush big enough for the Dixie™ cup and sit the cup in it so that ice comes up around the sides but doesn't get into the mixture.
6. Using the clean stir stick, stir the ice cream mixture slowly, scraping the newly formed crystals from the bottom and sides of the cup and stopping from time to time to let the ice cream harden.
   (You may have to stir on and off for 20 to 30 minutes until the ice cream is ready to eat-icy and only slightly soft.)
   *If you want to try flavors add a little chocolate syrup or other flavorings to the ice cream until slushy.

Protein

Meat, Poultry, Fish, Eggs, Beans

Welcome to the fifth section of the food pyramid. **Protein** is the main nutrient in this part of the pyramid plus minerals and the B vitamins, especially B12.

Meat ranks as high nutritionally as it does in popularity. The most favored meat is that from the steer or cow, called beef.

Meat is a p**rotein**. The word meat comes from the Greek word meaning "first" or "of primary importance."

Protein
steak, hamburger, ham, pork chops, chicken, turkey, duck, fish, shrimp, eggs, drybeans such as black beans, black-eye peas, cranberry beans, lima beans, pinto beans, red beans, peas, chick-peas, lentils, soybeans, peanuts, walnuts, cashews, almonds, and seeds

What is meat? Our meats come from livestock, which are living animals. Cows, pigs, lambs, and chickens live on farms where they are raised on grass, grains, hay, or wheat.

When they grow big enough they are brought to the slaughterhouse and killed. The butcher cleans and cuts the meat. Then it is delivered to stores. Meat from all animals is used completely by the body, meaning that the protein and fat are used to help our bodies work.

Where do burgers dance?
At the meat ball.

2 -3 servings recommended. One serving is equal to two to three ounces of cooked, lean meat, poultry and fish; one egg; one-half cup cooked beans or two tablespoons of seeds or nuts.

Cheeseburger Pizza Bites *Makes 20*

I just love hamburgers; but hold the pickles. The hamburger made its first appearance at the St. Louis Purchase Exposition in 1904 and is now one of America's favorite foods. The name "hamburger" comes from the seaport town of Hamburg, Germany.

Things You'll Need

• cookie sheet • knife • skillet • spoon • grater

Ingredients

1 can (10 count) biscuits
2 teaspoons mustard
1 pound hamburger meat
1 teaspoon salt
1/4 teaspoon pepper
1 cup cheese, shredded
20 pickles, sliced
Purple onion, diced (optional)

1. Prepare the biscuits according to package directions, cool and cut in half.
2. While the biscuits are cooking, place the hamburger meat in a skillet and cook until brown, drain the fat. Sprinkle with seasonings.
3. Place the biscuits cut side up on the cutting boards and lightly spread with the mustard, top with the hamburger meat and shredded cheese.
4. Place the biscuits back on the cookie sheet and place them in the oven to melt the cheese.
5. Remove from the oven and top with the pickle slice.

Beef Jerky

Things You'll Need:

• knife and cutting board • glass bowl

Ingredients:

1 pound lean, boneless meat
2 tablespoons soy sauce
1 teaspoon Worcestershire sauce
1/4 teaspoon pepper
1/4 teaspoon garlic powder
1/4 teaspoon onion powder
1/2 teaspoon hickory smoke

1. Trim fat from meat and cut to 1/8 to 1/4 inch slices.
2. Place remaining ingredients in a glass bowl.
3. Place meat strips into the marinade and marinate for 1 hour.
4. Preheat the oven to 200 degrees. Shake off excess liquid and lay the meat on racks in the oven.
5. Dry the meat at the lowest possible temperature until it turns brown, feels hard, and is dry to the touch. This will take from 4 to 7 hours.
6. Remove and pat off the excess oil, let the meat cool. Store in an airtight container in a cool place.

Eggs-ventures are exciting.

Eggs are laid by chickens on farms or in-fenced yards.
When farmers remove the eggs for people to eat, hens keep laying more.

Chicken eggs are white or brown. Small greenish eggs come from pheasants, big white eggs are laid by geese, and speckled eggs come from wild turkeys.

Protein-rich eggs are a favorite breakfast food. Used in baking, they color a cake with a rich natural yellow and help hold foods together in cooking. Eggs marks the spot!

Name of Activity

Things You'll Need

▪ 1 hard boiled egg ▪ knife ▪ 1 raw egg ▪ plate

What are the parts of an egg?

There is a hard shell on the outside of the egg. Look at the shell through a magnifying glass. What do you see? The shell is not smooth. It has many bumps and dents. It also has invisible holes that let air move in and out. Next, peel the shell off a hard-boiled egg. Cut the egg in half along its length. What do you find inside?

The egg has four parts. Right under the shell there is a thin, rubbery skin. It is the egg membrane. The white of the egg is the albumen. The last part is the yellow center. It is the egg yolk. Speaking of eggs, What do you call a mischievous egg? A practical yolker.

Crack an egg into an empty dish. When you crack an egg you see a clear liquid around a yellow blob. What does heat do to the liquid parts of the egg? With the help of a grown-up, fry the liquid insides of an egg in a pan. Try not to break the yellow part. What happens when the pan gets hot?

The clear liquid changes quickly into a white solid. That is why the clear liquid is known as the white of the egg. Next, cover the pan. After about 5 minutes lift the cover and look at the egg. What do you see? The yellow part has also changed from a liquid to a solid.

Devotion: *The egg is safe and secure in its shell. When we put our trust in God we have the security of His love. Even when the days are hard we know that God loves and cares for us.*

LORD, you have assigned me my portion and my cup; you have made my lot secure. Therefore my heart is glad and my tongue rejoices; my body also will rest secure. **Psalm 16:5, 9**

It's the **Poultry Place**. Chickens, turkeys, ducks, geese, and rock Cornish hens are all domesticated birds bred and raised for us to eat.

These birds are high in **protein** and low in **fat**. Chicken is the most often used bird in the poultry family. Before cooking they are cleaned and plucked, some are de-boned and some are left whole. You can buy chicken fresh, frozen, canned, and in soups, stews and spreads.

It is a good source of calcium, phosphorus, and iron and contains riboflavin, thiamin, and niacin.

Barbecue Chicken Pops *Makes 16 pops*

Things You'll Need

• Cutting board • knife • skewers • cookie sheet
• medium plastic resealable bag• measuring spoons • pastry brush

Ingredients

4 chicken breast, skinless and boneless
1 cup barbecue sauce
1 cup bread crumbs
1 teaspoon salt
1/4 teaspoon pepper
1/4 teaspoon onion salt

1. Place the chicken breast on the cutting board and cut into 4 sections.
2. Spray a cookie sheet with cooking spray, place the cut chicken on the cookie sheet.
3. Thread the pieces of cut chicken onto the skewers.
4. Brush the chicken on both sides with the barbecue sauce.
5. Place the bread crumbs and seasonings into the plastic bag, close the bag and shake to combine all the ingredients. Add the chicken and shake until the pieces are thoroughly coated.
6. Pick the chicken pieces up using the skewers and place on a cookie sheet.
7. Place in a 350 degree oven and bake for 15 to 17 minutes.
   Serve with warm barbecue sauce.

This is the **Bean** Scene!

Dry beans, peas, and nuts–are similar to meat in terms of the **protein** they provide but they also add **fiber** to our diets.

Delicate pea and bean flowers on climbing vines mature into fruit. Peas and beans grow in pocket-like pods, which are shells for the plants seeds. Removed from their pods and dried, legumes can keep for years. Legumes include chick-peas, lentils, soybeans, and peanuts which are not nuts, but peas.

Homemade Peanut Butter

Things You'll Need

• food processor • measuring cups

Ingredients

2 cups peanuts, 1 teaspoon salt

1. Add the two cups of peanuts to the food processor and process until butter forms add salt and process until thoroughly mixed.
2. Store in an airtight container and refrigerate after opening.

Beans are important **protein** sources in many countries around the world. People called vegetarians do not eat meat for spiritual or health reasons, but rely on the beans, peas and nuts to provide part of their protein.

When is a hamburger not a hamburger? When it is made out of soybeans. Soybeans can be put into machines and shaped into all kinds of meat look-alikes, including bacon, chicken, and hamburger. How many types of beans are there?

Activity

Things You'll Need

▪ Assorted dried beans from the grocery store. Examples: black beans, black-eye peas, chick-peas, cranberry beans, lima beans, pinto beans, red beans, soybeans.

▪ glue ▪ heavy paper plates ▪ markers

Look at all the beans available in the grocery store today. At the top of your paper plate write the servings suggested by the food pyramid for the best amount of beans to be in your diet. Then make a collage using the beans.

Devotion: *Most dried beans must be soaked and picked through before cooking. The soaking softens the shell. The beans are picked through so the bad ones will not be eaten. Sometimes in our lives we have to deal with difficult people or bad beans. Dealing with people who are not nice to you can be very hard. God has asked us to pray for these people.*

But I tell you: Love your enemies and pray for those who persecute you. ***Matthew 5:44***

Bean Dip and Burrito Chips

Things You'll Need:
• cutting board • knife • large cookie sheet • pastry brush • 2 bowls
• large spoon • saucepan

Bean Dip Ingredients:
1 can refried beans
1 cup cheddar cheese, shredded
1/4 cup onion, finely diced

1. In a small saucepan combine all ingredients, stir to combine.
2. Heat for 4 to 5 minutes or until heated through.
3. Place in a serving bowl and serve with burrito chips.

Burrito Chips Ingredients:
4 large tortillas
butter, melted
1 teaspoon salt

1. On a cutting board, cut the tortilla into 8 sections, to resemble a pie.
2. Place the tortillas on the cookie sheet and brush each tortilla section with the melted butter. Sprinkle with salt.
3. Place in a 400 degree oven and bake for 8 minutes or until browned around the edges.

I think I smell something fishy. Freshwater **fish** live in lakes and streams. Saltwater fish share their ocean homes with many other sea creatures like shrimp, lobsters, squid, and mussels. Fish are cold-blooded animals covered with shiny scales. Breathing through gills, they feed underwater on plankton, insects, or small fish.

Fish are caught with lines or nets. Before cooking, they are cleaned, and the scales are scraped off. Fish are sold, frozen, canned, dried, or smoked.

Activity

Things You'll Need
- Pictures of fresh water and salt water fish from magazines or from the Internet.
- Paper, pencils, scissors.

Let each child choose a fish picture and write or tell a story about where the fish is found, like in the ocean, in the lake, or at hatcheries. Share the pictures and stories with friends or classmates.

Fish Fingers

Things You'll Need:

• measuring cup • small mixing bowl • nonstick cookie sheet • measuring spoons • timer • dinner plate • fork or wire whisk • resealable plastic storage bag • knife • cutting board

Ingredients:

1 pound boneless, skinless cod
1 egg white
1/4 cup milk
1 cup bread crumbs
1 teaspoon pepper
1 teaspoon dried parsley
1/4 teaspoon paprika
1 lemon, cut into wedges

1. Preheat the oven to 400 degrees.
2. Cut the fish into 8 stick-shaped pieces. Try to make them as even as possible.
3. Combine the egg and milk in a small bowl and briskly whip with a fork or wire whisk until foamy. (About 20 stokes)
4. Place the bread crumbs in the plastic bag. Add the seasonings and pour out onto a plate.
5. Dip the fish into the egg mixture, coat with the crumb mixture and place on the cookie sheet. Repeat this until all the fish is coated.
6. Squeeze the lemon juice over the fish sticks.
7. Place in the oven and bake for 20 minutes.

Devotion: *Jesus often used stories or parables to help people to understand how they should live. The disciples were fisherman and therefore knew the value of fish and the value of being fishers of men. Telling people about Jesus, made them fishers of men.*

Christians, at the sign of a fish drawn in the sand recognized other Christians. This was like a secret code. Remember how the little boy fed a whole crowd with his loaves and fishes? Boy, Jesus really used him.

As Jesus walked beside the Sea of Galilee, he saw Simon and his brother Andrew casting a net into the lake, for they were fishermen. "Come, follow me," Jesus said, "and I will make you fishers of men." At once they left their nets and followed him. ***Mark 1, 16-18***

Fats, Oils and Sweets

We are at our final station of the pyramid. The very tip top is where you find **Fats, Oils, and Sweets**. For many of us, the majority of our calories come from this section. The goal of the food pyramid is to change that and help us to eat a better more balanced diet.

Fats, Oils & Sweets
sweets such as
pastries, cakes, pies,
cookies, donuts, sugars,
soft drinks, and candies;
salads dressings and oils,
butter, margarine,
fried foods
such as french fries,
potato chips

Foods like salad dressings and oils, cream, butter, margarine, sugars, soft drinks, candies, and sweet desserts provide calories but give little nutrition. To be at your healthiest use this section a little at a time.

Fats are important nutrients to maintain body functions. They are used for energy and to keep you warm. Fats give you a feeling of being full. They are the slowest of all foods to be digested. Fats give a steady, slow-burning fuel to your cells.

My friend **Fats** helps the body absorb **vitamins** A, D, E, K and beta-carotene. They help slow sugar's release into the bloodstream and are important for the formation of cell membranes.

Fast food or fat food is sometimes called junk food. This makes it sound as if it fills you up without supplying any nutrients, which is not always true. Fast food is not bad for you unless you eat it very often and do not eat a variety of other foods.

**Servings Recommended:
Use sparingly**

Feasting on Fat Activity

Things You'll Need:

▪ a large brown paper bag ▪ scissors ▪ pens or markers ▪ several different kinds of food (french fries, potato chips, carrots, milk, and apple juice)

1. Cut the bag into 3-inch squares. Label each square with the name of one of the foods you have.
2. Rub some of each food or put a few drops of the liquid on the square labeled with its name.
3. Let the square dry.
4. When dry, hold each square up to a light. What effect did different foods have on the paper?

The spots where the light shines through the paper show that f**at** has been absorbed. Different substances let light pass through at different speeds. Whenever light travels from one substance to another and changes speeds abruptly, some of it gets scattered. Paper is made of many strands of fiber, with air between them. Because light travels through air at different speeds, most of the light gets scattered as it goes from air to fiber and very little gets through.

Light travels through f**at** and f**iber** at very similar speeds. When fat soaks into the air spaces between the fibers that make up the paper, light can pass through the paper without as much scattering, turning your brown paper squares into fat detectors.

***Devotion** : It is hard to eat donuts and french fries in small amounts because they taste so good. When you put limits on your eating you are learning an important lesson called discipline. Your parents will discipline you to help you understand right from wrong. This helps you set limits in your life. God disciplines His children for the same reasons.*

When we are judged by the Lord, we are being disciplined so that we will not be condemned with the world. ***1 Corinthians 11:32***

There are several different parts of my family. **Saturated Fats** are mostly found in animal products and in some tropical plant oils. You can tell that a fat is saturated because it usually hardens at a low room temperature. Some examples are butter, cream, lard, coconut oil and palm oil.

Fat is a nutrient needed daily for fuel, energy, growth, and health.

Homemade Buttermilk Dressing *Makes 1 cup*

Things You'll Need:
• measuring cups and spoons • whisk or spoon for stirring • bowl or container with lid

Ingredients:

1 cup mayonnaise
1 cup buttermilk
1 tablespoon Parmesan cheese, grated
1 tablespoon fresh chives, chopped
1/4 teaspoon garlic salt
1/4 teaspoon pepper

1. Combine mayonnaise and buttermilk and stir.
2. Stir in cheese and seasonings.
3. Cover and store in the refrigerator for up to two weeks.

Unsaturated Fats are from plants. They are best known as oils. Some examples are olive oil, corn oil, peanut oil, and cod liver oil. We need these oils for healthy skin and for our nervous system but they still must be eaten in small amounts.

Fries are very fatty, although they also supply energy, **protein** and **vitamin C**.

French Fries

Things You'll Need:
• cutting board • knife • deep and wide pot

Ingredients:
4 medium potatoes, oil, salt

1. Wash and cut the potatoes into long strips.
2. Pour the oil into the pot and heat.
3. When the oil is heated, carefully drop the potato strips into the oil, cook until brown.

How Sweet It Is! Sugar gives you energy but it has no other nutrients besides **carbohydrates**. Sugar is a simple carbohydrate. Sugars are naturally found in foods like milk or fruit and are added to foods like candy.

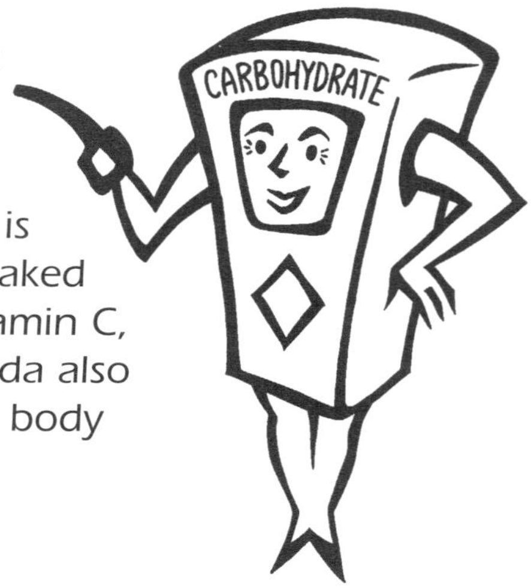

Sugars have lots of calories, but practically no vitamins, minerals, or other valuable nutrients. They contain what is called an "empty calorie." For example a medium-sized baked potato has 100 calories, and lots of nutrients such as vitamin C, protein, iron, phosphorus, and more. But 6 ounces of soda also have 100 calories, mostly in sugar, but little else that our body needs for good health.

Sugar Sweet and Crystal Clear Activity

Things You'll Need:

▪ 12 -inch piece of string ▪ straw ▪ paper clip ▪ glass jar ▪ magnifying lens ▪ small saucepan ▪ 1 cup water ▪ 2 cups sugar

1. Put one cup of water in the saucepan. Place on high heat and bring to a boil.
2. Add sugar and stir until no more sugar will dissolve.
3. Remove the saucepan from the burner and turn the heat off. Cool for 10 minutes.
4. Tie one end of the string to the straw. Tie the paper clip to the other end of the string so that the clip just dangles above the bottom of the jar when the straw is placed over the top of the jar.
5. Drop the end of the string with the paper clip into the jar and lay the straw across the top of the jar.
6. Pour the sugar water into the jar. Put the jar in place where it won't be disturbed for seven days.
7. Look at the jar with your magnifying lens. What do you find?

Devotion: *Dear God, just as I see every detail of the sugar crystal, You see every part of my heart. Help me live my life so that what You see makes You happy.*

Search me, O God, and know my heart; test me and know my anxious thoughts. See if there is any offensive way in me, and lead me in the way everlasting. ***Psalm 139:23-24***

There are many different forms of sugar at the supermarket: white sugar, brown sugar, powdered or confectioners' sugar, corn syrup, and molasses.

There are really only two basic kinds of sugar; **natural sugar** and **refined sugars**. Natural sugars occur naturally in foods, like honey. Refined sugars have to be man-made.

Honey is the oldest source of sweetness known to humans. This sweet thick liquid is made by bees. Bees sip a liquid called nectar from flowers to help them make honey. The bees then carry this nectar back to their hives in a pouch in their bodies.

The nectar in the pouch breaks down into fructose and glucose. The bees store the sugar mixture in tiny cells, in their hives. There the water and sugar mixture evaporates and what is left turns to honey.

Honey contains a small amount of **minerals** your body needs, including potassium, calcium, and phosphorus. For this reason many people use honey instead of artificial sweeteners.

Devotion: *Dear God, the Bible says that Your rules and directions for our lives are as sweet as honey. You promise to reward me when I obey Your rules. You even promise to help me do this if I pray and ask You to forgive my sins and help me do what's right.*

They are more precious than gold, than much pure gold; they are sweeter than honey, than honey from the comb. **Psalm 19:10**

Fructose is called a fruit sugar because it occurs naturally in fruits. Refined light sugars are usually white, the most common and cheapest sugar is called granulated sugar or table sugar. Table sugar is what you sprinkle on your breakfast cereal.

Vanilla Sugar Activity

Things You'll Need:

▪ 2 cups granulated sugar ▪ vanilla bean ▪ air tight container

Instructions:

1. Pour the sugar into the container and the vanilla bean.
2. Screw the lid on tightly.
3. Shake the container of sugar and set aside for a few days.
4. Open the container and you will find that the sugar has taken on the smell of vanilla. This type of sugar works well in baking and stirring into drinks.

Sugar as a preservative is often added to foods for taste, but sometimes it performs another function: sugar can act as a preservative to help foods from spoiling. It is often included in packaged foods and drinks to make them last longer. It is important to find out which foods contain sugar, because you may be eating more sugar that you realize.

Sugar Spotter Activity

Things You'll Need:

▪ paper ▪ pencil ▪ can of favorite food
▪ can of favorite soda or juice

Instructions:

1. Make 3 columns on your notebook paper. Label the columns 1) Food 2) Sweet 3) Does it contain sugar?
2. Carefully read the ingredient label on your favorite canned or packaged food and your favorite drink. See if sugar is listed.
3. If the ingredients don't include sugar see if the words sucrose, fructose, glucose, maltose, or lactose is listed. These mean sugar too.
Make a list of the foods and drinks you've looked at. Note whether they taste sweet and if they contain sugar.

Devotion: *Dear God, just like it is easy to eat something without knowing everything that's inside it, it can be easy to get into problems before I realize it. Help me to remember to ask for Your help and to study Your Bible so I will make wise choices.*

Your word is a lamp to my feet and a light for my path. **Psalm 119:105**

Real Saltwater Taffy

Try these recipes from the sweets section of our Pyramid Cafe.

Things You'll Need:
• medium-sized saucepan • candy thermometer
• 8x8x2 square pan • wax paper • measuring cups and spoons • glass of ice water • kitchen scissors

Ingredients:
1 cup sugar
3/4 cup light corn syrup
2/3 cup salt
(fresh water with 1 teaspoon salt)
1 tablespoon cornstarch
2 tablespoons sweet butter
2 tablespoons vanilla
3 to 4 drops red food coloring

1. Mix all the ingredients in a medum-sized saucepan.
2. Cook over medium heat, stirring constantly until the mixture reaches 260 degrees on a candy thermometer, or until a bit of the mixture dropped into iced water forms into a hard ball.
3. Remove from the heat and pour into a buttered 8X8X2 inch square pan.
4. Allow to cool slightly, and then pull the taffy until shiny, stiff, and light in color. If the taffy begins to get too sticky, butter hands lightly. Pull into long strips about 1/2-inch wide.
5. Using scissors, cut into 1-inch pieces and wrap them individually in waxed paper. Keep in an airtight container.

Pine-Orange-Banana Balls

Things You'll Need:
• food processor • large plastic bag • rolling pin • large bowl • teaspoon

Ingredients
1 box vanilla wafers, 1 small can pine-orange-banana juice, 1 box powdered sugar

1. Crush wafers in a food processor, or put them in a large plastic bag and roll over them with a rolling pin until they are finely crushed.
2. In a large bowl, combine crushed wafers, juice, and powdered sugar. Stir until thoroughly combined.
3. Let the dough stand for about 30 minutes.
4. Scoop the dough out with a teaspoon and roll into balls.
5. Place balls in an air-tight container until ready to serve.

What grows on trees, is shaped like a melon and is full of beans? Cacao pods, used to make the world's favorite treat - chocolate.

Homemade Chocolate Bar

Things You'll Need:
• double boiler • wax paper • water

Ingredients
2 tablespoons powdered cocoa
2 tablespoons table sugar or fruit sugar (fructose)
1 teaspoon unsalted butter or vegetable shortening

1. Put enough water in the bottom of the double boiler to just touch the top half when its in place.
2. Remove the top half and bring the water to a boil on the stove.
3. Turn off the heat and put the top half of the double boiler into place.
4. Put the cocoa, sugar, and butter or shortening together into the top of the double boiler and stir until the mixture is smooth and the sugar is dissolved.
5. Spread the wax paper on a counter near the stove.
6. Carefully remove the top of the double boiler and pour the chocolate mixture onto the wax paper. Let it harden and taste.

*If you made your first batch with table sugar try making it again and use the fruit sugar this time.

Which do you prefer? Can you taste a difference between the two sugars?

Conclusion of the Pyramid Cafe Tour

Now its your turn. My kitchen is now yours to use. It is your chance to create healthy meals. You are the honored guest chef of the Pyramid Cafe. Put on your chef coat and toque (chef hat) and begin using what you have learned from your tour of the Pyramid Cafe. By the way, do you know what a tightrope walker eats? A balanced diet!

Meals for the Day Activity

Here's your chance to plan a day of fabulous meals from soup to nuts. Think about all the stations we visited in the Pyramid Cafe kitchen while planning the day's meals. It is best to consider all of the meals for the day. Make sure that the foods you choose add up to the recommended amounts from each of the basic food groups.

For example, if you have an egg for breakfast you only need one serving of meat, fish, or poultry the rest of the day. This is what is meant by eating a balanced diet.

Things You'll Need

- heavy paper plates (three per person) ▪ scissors
- glue ▪ food pictures from magazines

Instructions:

1. Take the 3 paper plates and label the tops of the plates with breakfast, lunch, and dinner.
2. Cut out food pictures from the magazines that show foods that you would eat for breakfast, lunch, and dinner.
3. Be sure to get foods from each section of the pyramid.
4. Plan a "good for you" selection of foods and paste your food pictures onto the paper plates.

Be sure and keep in mind that casseroles and salads combine foods from several of the food groups. So, chew on that for a while!

Devotion: *Dear God, You say my body is Your home here. Help me to care for it the way You want me to.*

Therefore, I urge you, brothers, in view of God's mercy, to offer your bodies as living sacrifices, holy and pleasing to God--this is your spiritual act of worship. Do not conform any longer to the pattern of this world, but be transformed by the renewing of your mind. Then you will be able to test and approve what God's will is--his good, pleasing and perfect will. **Romans 12:1-2**

Things to remember when you are planning meals:
▪ Select a main dish from the meat group. ▪ Add a bread or maybe a rice dish to go with the meat dish. ▪ Choose a hot or cold vegetable. ▪ Select a fruit or vegetable salad that goes with the meat. ▪ Choose a beverage, this is a great place to use the dairy group. ▪ If you like add a dessert, fruits and milk-based desserts are good choices to help meet the recommended foods from each section. After you have met the basic requirements listed on the pyramid, you can add the extras.

Name that Food Group Activity

Many foods you eat are made up of more than one food group. See if you can name the food groups in these everyday foods. Just write the number in the circle provided for each group.

1. Carbohydrate
2. Vegetable
3. Fruit
4. Dairy
5. Protein

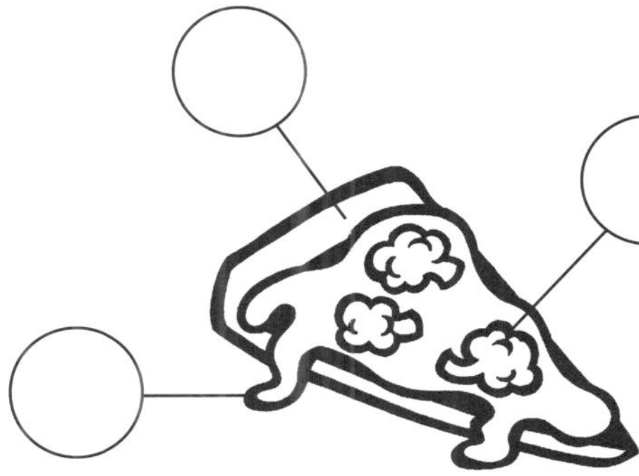

A

B

C

D

Answers (left to right): A - 4,1,2
B - 1,4,3 C - 1,2,5,2 D - 4,3,1

Place in the Pyramid Activity

Things You'll Need:

- pencil
- reproduced page of food pictures and pyramid sections

Instructions:

Draw a line from each food to the food group it belongs to.

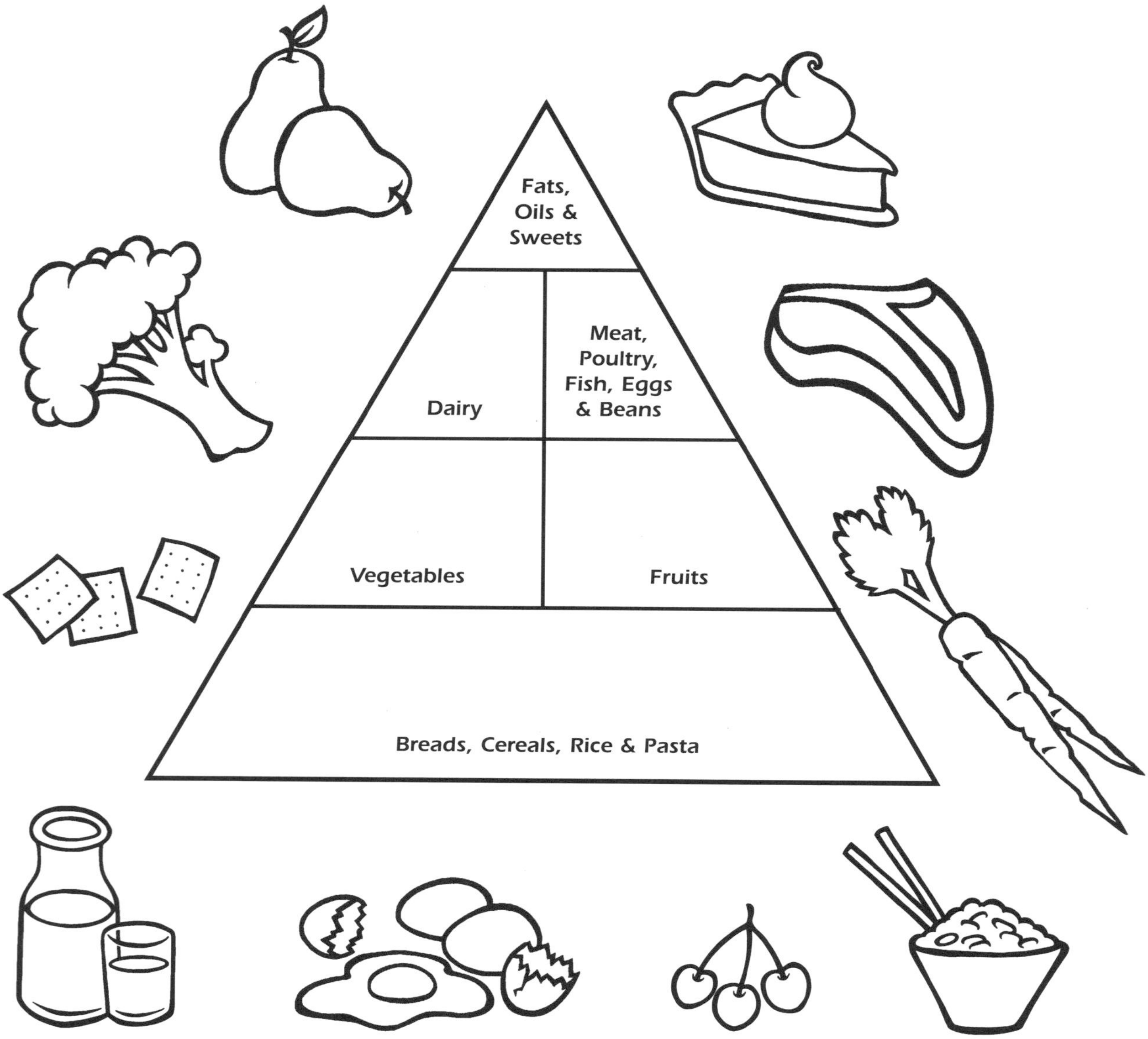

I hope you have enjoyed the tour of the Pyramid Cafe. God created our bodies to be moving miracles. Our choice is to make the most of our miracle by eating the right kinds of foods. I hope you use the Pyramid Cafe to guide you as you make decisions on what to eat each day.

So whether you eat or drink or whatever you do, do it all for the glory of God. **1 Corinthians 10:31**

The Pyramid Cafe

Presents

EAT FOR GOOD HEALTH

CERTIFICATE

This certifies that

____

(write your name here)

knows about the
great foods that God
has provided from
the Food Pyramid and
how to make
healthy food choices.

____

Parent or teacher signature